The Sleepy Old Lady
In the Park

Stephanie Hanouw

ELM HILL

A Division of
HarperCollins Christian Publishing

www.elmhillbooks.com

© 2019 Stephanie Hanouw

**The Sleepy Old Lady
In the Park**

All rights reserved. No portion of this book may be reproduced, stored in a retrieval system, or transmitted in any form or by any means—electronic, mechanical, photocopy, recording, scanning, or other—except for brief quotations in critical reviews or articles, without the prior written permission of the publisher.

Published in Nashville, Tennessee, by Elm Hill, an imprint of Thomas Nelson. Elm Hill and Thomas Nelson are registered trademarks of HarperCollins Christian Publishing, Inc.

Elm Hill titles may be purchased in bulk for educational, business, fund-raising, or sales promotional use. For information, please e-mail SpecialMarkets@ThomasNelson.com.

Publisher's Note: This novel is a work of fiction. Names, characters, places, and incidents are either products of the author's imagination or used fictitiously. All characters are fictional, and any similarity to people living or dead is purely coincidental.

Library of Congress Cataloging-in-Publication Data

Library of Congress Control Number: 2019910450

ISBN 978-1-400326495 (Paperback)
ISBN 978-1-400326501 (Hardbound)
ISBN 978-1-400326518 (eBook)

Dedicated to my loving, encouraging mother and father who are story makers in their own rights!

As the sun begins to slip silently down behind the mountains, it leaves a trail of orange, yellow, pink, and purple on the evening sky. It's time for the sleepy old lady to get up from her favorite rickety bench and start toward home. She often visits the park at the end of a busy day to relax and look at the beautiful plants and animals that God made. But now it's time to go home. She gets up, stretches out her arms, and yawns a very big yawn, then off she goes.

As she walks, she comes to a very stickery raspberry bush. Hiding underneath is a little gray bunny which hops onto her path.

"Can you play with me?" the bunny asks the sleepy old lady.

"Oh, not now, my friend," she replies. "I am too sleepy. I must go home to my nice, cozy, comfy bed." Then she lifts her hand to cover a great big yawn.

She walks on toward the small pond where families of friendly ducks swim peacefully in quiet circles. One fluffy duckling swims quickly to the pond's muddy edge. Hurrying to the smooth rock beside the old lady's path, he waddles to the top, stretching up on his tiny webbed toes.

"Can you play with me?" the fuzzy duckling quacks to the sleepy old lady.

"Oh, not now, my friend," she replies. "I am too sleepy. I must go home to my nice, cozy, comfy bed." Then she lifts her hand to cover *another* great big yawn.

The sleepy old lady walks on, breathing in the sweet fragrance of the tiny jasmine flowers growing beside her path. A beautiful butterfly, which had been resting on a dainty yellow blossom, flutters down close to her ear.

"Can you play with me?" the butterfly whispers to the sleepy old lady. (Butterflies are very quiet you know.)

"Oh, not now, my friend," replies the sleepy old lady. "I am too sleepy. I must go home to my nice, cozy, comfy bed." Then she lifts her hand to cover *one more* great big yawn.

At the top of the next rise, the sleepy old lady smiles as a graceful dove lands gently upon her shoulder.

"Can you play with me?" coos the dove to the sleepy old lady.

"Oh, not now, my friend," replies the sleepy old lady. "I am too sleepy. I must go home to my nice, cozy, comfy bed." Then she lifts her hand to cover *yet another* great big yawn.

The sleepy old lady arrives at her door just as the colorful evening sky turns into a velvety starry night. She enters her snug little house, and walks wearily to her bathroom. Changing into her favorite pajamas, she washes her wrinkly face, combs her silvery hair, and then brushes her pearly teeth. Finally, she is ready for bed.

With a smile, she folds back her lovely quilt and fluffs her pillow so it lay plump and inviting upon her soft, clean sheets. She climbs into bed, pulls up her cozy covers, and turns off her bedside lamp.

She closes her sleepy eyes and covers one last great big yawn. As she drifts off to sleep, she whispers, "Good night, all of my wonderful friends. God bless you."

Printed in the USA
CPSIA information can be obtained
at www.ICGtesting.com
LVHW060830241123
764757LV00043B/69